Our Moon Journey

We traveled far, far away
beyond the star-lighted Pacific
over the nine dragon mountains of Hong Kong
across the rice paddies of Guangdong
down the wide Pearl River.
And we drank tea in Maoming
beside ten nannies
with ten babies
from Xinyi.
Then she was ours.
So we adopted her
on a July day
in 1997.
—K.H.C.

For Margaret, who waited patiently, and for Chinese Children Adoption, who helped us find her —K.

For my parents, John and Joan —P.B.

THIS IS A BORZOI BOOK
PUBLISHED BY ALFRED A. KNOPF • Text copyright
© 2010 by Karen Henry Clark • Illustrations copyright
© 2010 by Patrice Barton • All rights reserved. Published in
the United States by Alfred A. Knopf, an imprint of Random House
Children's Books, a division of Random House, Inc., New York. • Knopf,
Borzoi Books, and the colophon are registered trademarks of Random House,
Inc. • Visit us on the Web! www.randomhouse.com/kids • Educators and librarians,
for a variety of teaching tools, visit us at www.randomhouse.com/teachers • Library of
Congress Cataloging-in-Publication Data • Clark, Karen Henry. • Sweet moon baby / by Karen
Henry Clark ; illustrations by Patrice Barton. — 1st ed. • p. cm. • Summary: The smiling moon
watches over a baby girl in China whose parents love her but cannot take care of her, and guides
a childless couple that lives far away to the daughter for whom they yearn. • ISBN 978-0-375-
85709-6 (trade) — ISBN 978-0-375-95709-3 (lib. bdg.) • [1. Adoption—Fiction. 2. Moon—Fiction.]
I. Barton, Patrice, ill. II. Title. • PZ7.C5479Swe 2010 [E]—dc22 2009018343 • The illustrations
in this book were created digitally with pencil sketches scanned into Corel Painter software. •
MANUFACTURED IN CHINA • December 2010 • 10 9 8 7 6 5 4 3 2 1 • First Edition • Random
House Children's Books supports the First Amendment and celebrates the right to read.

SWEET MOON BABY

An Adoption Tale

Written by Karen Henry Clark • Illustrated by Patrice Barton

Alfred A. Knopf New York

On a summer night in China, a baby girl was born.
She was perfect.

"We have barely enough rice to feed ourselves," the father said.

"She should have pretty things," the mother said.

"She should learn to read," the father said.

They were happy and sad at the same time.

From high in the warm sky, the moon's face glowed on the river,
making a path as clear as the night's promise.

In time the mother said, "We must trust the moon. Only good things
will happen to our daughter." So they placed her in a basket.

"Will she remember us?" the father asked.

"Somehow," the mother answered.

They whispered good-bye to their tiny girl, and she floated away.

Still, she slept.

Then the river grew shallow. She was caught in the mud. A turtle saw
her in the moonlight and carried her to deeper water.

Still, she slept.

A sudden wind blew through the valley. She rocked dangerously in the waves. A peacock flew her to safety, singing a lullaby under the moon's watchful eyes.

Still, she slept.

Rain began to fall. A monkey jumped onto her basket. He kept her dry as they sailed for miles and miles beneath the smiling moon.

Still, she slept.

The river cut through the mountains, and swirling rapids surrounded her. A panda pulled her free. The moon's trail led them to gentle water.

Still, she slept.

Downstream the river dropped over a ledge. Fish raced to the surface
to catch her. Soaring over the rocks together, they landed on the moon's
glittering reflection.

Still, she slept.

On the other side of the world, a husband and wife could not sleep.
They wanted a daughter.

Still, she never came.

They made a garden to keep busy while they waited for her.

"Maybe she will like carrots," the wife said.

"Maybe she will like peas," the husband said.

Still, she never came.

Next they planted fruit trees.

In case she likes pie," the wife said.

In case she likes climbing," the husband said.

Still, she never came.

They built a house with a room just for her.

"Perhaps she will like pretty things," the wife said.

"Perhaps she will like books," the husband said.

They were happy and sad at the same time.

One night they looked up at the moon's kind face.

"It sees her," the wife said.

"We must find her," the husband said.

So they hoped for a sign telling them where
to look for their little one.

They chased a shooting star across the midnight sky. She was not there.

They followed the next one as it flashed beside the moon.

She was not there either.

They searched moonlit flower beds. She was not with the ferns or roses. She was not in the daisies.

They crisscrossed a hundred roads. Coins twinkling like scattered moonbeams took them from corner to corner. But she was not at any turn.

They covered great distances indeed.

At last they sailed down a shimmering path on a wide river.

"Faster, faster," they whispered into the current.

Then there she was, their sweet moon baby, waiting for them among the water lilies. She opened her eyes to see the smiling faces of her mother and father.

They carried her home,

where she grows strong and true
on carrots, peas, and pie,

where she plays with
pretty things,

where she reads high up
in a cherry tree.

And as she sleeps soundly, whenever the moon is full, she dreams of a baby girl born on a summer night in China.